To Betsy
— DC

To John William Reilly.
Welcome to the world.
— BL

SIMON AND SCHUSTER • First published in Great Britain in 2009 by Simon & Schuster UK Ltd, 1st Floor, 222 Gray's Inn Road, London, WC1X 8HB • A CBS COMPANY • Originally published in 2008 by Atheneum Books for Young Readers, an imprint of Simon & Schuster Children's Publishing Division, New York • Text copyright © 2008 Doreen Cronin • Illustrations copyright © 2008 Betsy Lewin • All rights reserved. • The rights of Doreen Cronin and Betsy Lewin to be identified as the author and illustrator of this work have been asserted by them in accordance with the Copyright, Designs and Patents Act, 1988 • All rights reserved including the right of reproduction in whole or in part in any form • A CIP catalogue record for this book is available from the British Library upon request. • ISBN: 978 1 84738 472 0 • Printed in Singapore • 10 9 8 7 6 5 4 3 2 1

Thump, Quack, Moo

A Whacky Adventure

by **Doreen Cronin**
and **Betsy Lewin**

SIMON AND SCHUSTER
LONDON   NEW YORK   SYDNEY

It is almost time for the annual Corn Maze Festival.

Farmer Brown is very excited.

This year he is making a Statue of Liberty corn maze.

He is going to need help to get everything ready on time.

The chickens do not want to help.
"I'll let you use my hammers,"
said Farmer Brown.

The chickens are now building the fence around the corn field.

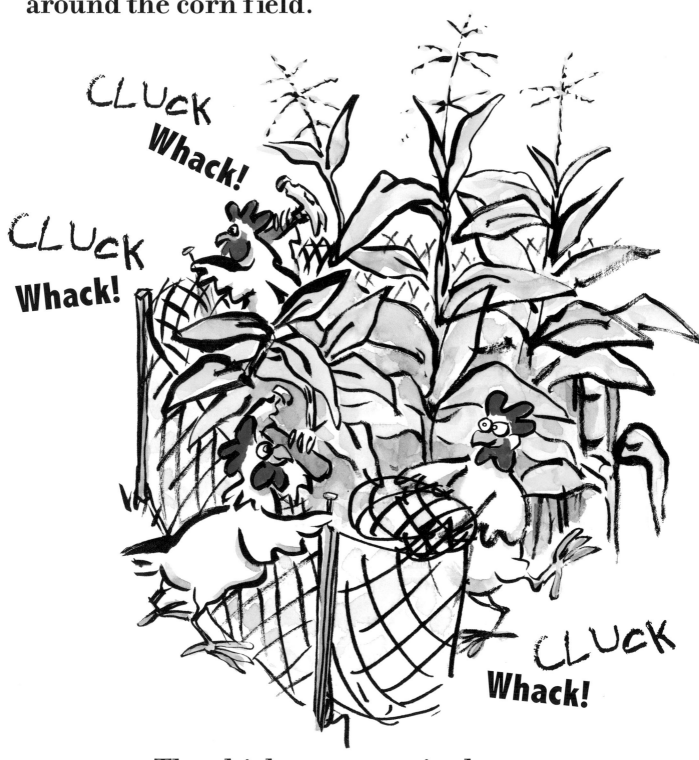

The chickens are excited.

The cows do not want to help.
"I'll let you use my paintbrushes,"
said Farmer Brown.

The cows are now giving the barn
a fresh coat of paint.

The cows are excited.

Duck never wants to help.
"No help," said Farmer Brown to Duck,
"no more special-order organic duck feed."

Thump

QUack.

Thump

Duck is still not excited.

The mice are taking a correspondence course on meteorology and are too busy to lend a hand.

The air is filled
with the busy sounds
of the farm.

Thump.

The mice keep an eye on the weather.

Farmer Brown is busy too.
Every day he gets out his
sketch book, graph paper,
art supplies and mower.

He sketches a little . . .

measures a little . . .

counts a little . . .

and cuts. Farmer Brown wants it perfect.

Every night Duck sneaks into the corn field.
He brings his sketch book, graph paper,
art supplies and hedge clippers.
He also brings his night-vision goggles
and glow-in-the-dark ruler.
Then he sketches a little . . .

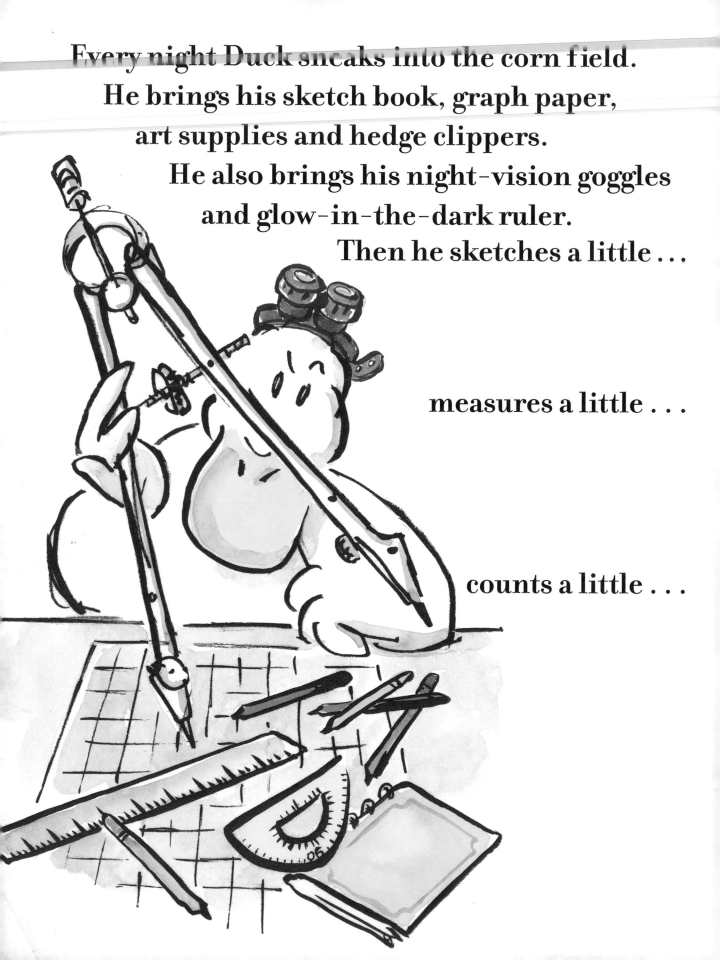

measures a little . . .

counts a little . . .

Thwack!

Thump.

The mice keep an eye
on the weather.

BAROMETRIC
PRESSURE
DROPPING

It is the day before the annual Corn Maze Festival. For the last time Farmer Brown gets out his sketch book, graph paper, art supplies and mower.

He sketches a little . . .
measures a little . . .
counts a little . . .
and cuts.

The Statue of Liberty corn maze is finished!
He is too excited to sleep.

Duck sneaks into the corn field for the last time. He brings his sketch book, graph paper, art supplies and hedge clippers. He also brings his night-vision goggles and glow-in-the-dark ruler.

Then he sketches a little . . .
measures a little . . .
counts a little . . .
and cuts.

He is too excited to sleep.

It is time for the Corn Maze Festival opening ceremony!

The chickens are not allowed to use the hammers anymore.

The barn is not quite what Farmer Brown had in mind.

The ticket stand has
a slight design flaw.

But all Farmer Brown cares about is the corn maze.

He pays five dollars and hops into the hot-air balloon.

At last he will see his masterpiecc from above!

Duck also pays five dollars and hops into the hot-air balloon.

At last he will see his masterpiece from above!

Duck is really excited now!

GERONIMO!

PARTLY CLOUDY, CHANCE OF DUCK